A Note to Parents and Teachers

SAINSBURY'S READING SCHEME is a compelling reading programme for children, designed in conjunction with leading literacy experts.

Action-packed, engaging, easy-to-read stories are complemented by vibrant illustrations to fire the imaginations of new readers. Each book in the SAINSBURY'S READING SCHEME is guaranteed to capture a child's interest while developing his or her reading skills, general knowledge and love of reading.

The five levels of the programme are aimed at different reading abilities, enabling you to choose the books that are exactly right for your child.

Yellow Level – Learning to read
Green Level – Beginning to read
Gold Level – Beginning to read alone
Ruby Level – Reading alone
Sapphire Level – Proficient readers

The "normal" age at which a child begins to read can be anywhere from three to eight years old, so these levels are only a general guideline.

No matter which level you select, you can be sure that you're helping children learn to read, then read to learn!

First published in Great Britain by HarperCollins *Children's Books* in 2009 as
Bug Buddies: Enemy Attack
This edition published in partnership with Sainsbury's Reading Scheme in 2014
HarperCollins *Children's Books* is a division of HarperCollins*Publishers* Ltd,
77-85 Fulham Palace Road, Hammersmith, London W6 8JB

Visit us on the web at
www.harpercollins.co.uk

1 3 5 7 9 10 8 6 4 2

Enemy Attack
Text © 2009 Working Partners Limited
Illustrations © 2009 and 2014 Duncan Smith
Series created by Working Partners

With special thanks to Mariam Vossough

ISBN 978-0-00-759496-2

Printed and bound in China

Sainsbury's
Reading Scheme

Ruby Level
Reading alone

Enemy Attack

Joe Miller

Illustrated by Duncan Smith

HarperCollins *Children's Books*

Spinner's Wood
is full of sticky mud, tall trees
and long grass. But most of
all, it's full of bugs! Now, some
people think that bugs are pests.
But they haven't met Gonzo or
the **Bug Buddies** – four best
friends called **Zap, Buzz,
Lurch** and **Crunch**. Their life
would be perfect if it wasn't
for a spider called **Spinner**,
who has eight legs and one
mission: to trap the whole wood
in his evil web. But you'll
soon find out that even
bugs can be heroes...

Contents

CHAPTER 1

Zap flew through the air, high above the treetops.

Two of his friends, Buzz and Crunch, sat on Gonzo's Rock, cheering as Zip squeezed his tiny weevil body through a small gap between two branches.

It's now or never, thought Zap. He
turned upside down, before flipping
the right way up again. Then, beating
his wings with all his might, he did
another barrel roll.

10

Buzz the ladybird flapped his wings.

"Wow," he said. "I've never seen any

weevil do **two** flips!"

"You're little but **so** brave," said

Crunch, a big but not-so-brave

stag beetle.

11

Zap smiled with delight as he landed beside them on the rock.

"Look what I've got," a voice sang out behind them.

Zap was pleased to see his best friend, Lurch the dung beetle, approaching. Lurch was holding the Acorn Cup. Ever since their team won the Beetle Ball final, they'd taken it in turns to look after the trophy.

"Yippee!" said Buzz. "It's my turn for the cup! I'm going to polish it so much that I can see all seven of my spots in it."

12

Buzz crawled over to get the trophy, but quickly backed away.

"What have you done to it?" he cried. "It smells **horrible!**"

"Oops," said Lurch, his face flushing red. "I left Ploppy inside."

Lurch reached in and pulled out a smooth, round dung ball.

"You've had that thing for ages," said Zap.

"Yeah," said Buzz. "Fresh poo is bad enough, but that thing… **Yuck!**"

"Ploppy is so squishy I use him as

13

my pillow," replied Lurch. "That's why poo's so great – you can roll it, eat it and sleep on it. You can do anything with poo!"

Zap laughed. He loved his crazy friend, even though he didn't share his passion for poo.

Zap saw that Buzz was licking his lips. He shook his head – the ladybird had obviously seen something he could eat. Buzz was about to go scuttling off when Gonzo the grasshopper jumped on to his rock.

"Wait there, Buzz," said Gonzo. He

14

looked very serious. "I need to talk to you all."

Zap's wings tingled nervously. He hoped that Spinner the evil spider wasn't on the prowl again.

"I'm taking my annual trip to Cowpat Pasture tomorrow," Gonzo began.

"Why?" asked Lurch.

"Remember," said Zap, "he always goes there at this time of year to feed on fresh new grass."

"But who's going to look after Spinner's Wood?" asked Crunch.

"You are," said Gonzo. "The Bug Buddies."

There was silence. "But we're not… I mean…" stammered Zap.

The wise old grasshopper looked deep into Zap's eyes. "I won't always be here to protect the wood," he said. "One day, someone else will have to take over. But for now, you only have to look after it for a bit – I'll be back the day after tomorrow."

Zap held his head up high. "Then don't worry," he said. "We'll look after the wood while you're away."

"Yeah!" said Buzz, standing shoulder to shoulder with Zap.

Lurch and Crunch nodded. Although Crunch didn't look quite so sure.

"Thanks," said Gonzo. "You must take extra care – there are some newborn frogs and grasshoppers in the wood."

"Plus a scary giant spider," mumbled Crunch.

"Don't worry," said Gonzo. "I shall teach you all some Bug Attack moves. But we'll have to hurry, because I'm leaving at dawn."

Zap gazed about as Gonzo

 18

prepared for their lesson. *Spinner's Wood is huge*, he thought. *And I'm only a little weevil. Can a bug as small as me really look after the whole wood?*

Then Zap remembered that he and his friends had defeated Spinner once already. If the spider returned, they would defeat him again!

CHAPTER 2

The Bug Buddies gathered round
Gonzo, eager to learn some Bug
Attack moves.

"You can protect yourselves in
different ways," said Gonzo. "Let's
start with Buzz."

Lurch chortled. "What's he going to

do – **eat** all the baddies?"

Gonzo gave the dung beetle a stern look. "This is serious," he said.

"Sorry," mumbled Lurch, shuffling his legs.

"Ladybirds can squirt an enemy with their poison," Gonzo explained. He turned to Buzz. "But you need good aim."

Gonzo rolled a small, brown pebble to the edge of his rock. He told Buzz to try and hit it. The ladybird giggled with glee as he fired shot after shot. But his oily, yellow poison hit

everything *except* the pebble.

I know a way to get him to concentrate, thought Zap.

"Pretend that pebble is Spinner," he told Buzz.

22

The smile fell from the ladybird's face. He pulled his wings tight to his body and narrowed his eyes as he took aim. This time Buzz hit the pebble right in the centre.

"Great shot, Buzz!" shouted Zap.

Next, it was Crunch's turn.

"Do I have to?" asked the stag beetle, staring at the ground. "I don't like fighting."

"You don't have to *fight*," replied Gonzo. "You can use your flying to distract enemies."

"I don't understand," said Crunch.

23

"Fly over to those pond-skaters," said Gonzo, pointing a leg towards Algae Pond.

Crunch took off and wobbled his way towards the insects gliding on the water.

Zap held his breath as he watched his friend fly through the branches. Would he make it? Sure enough, Crunch's head clipped a twig and he went spinning through the air.

"Look at that crazy beetle!" shouted one of the pond-skaters.

The group of pond-skaters pointed

 24

and laughed. But watching Crunch

made them so dizzy, they all fell over!

"What a wobbly way to defend

yourself," said Lurch, as Crunch flew

slowly back to join them.

"But you see what I mean," said

Gonzo. "Crunch's flying technique

makes an enemy dizzy. And they can't

attack you if they're falling on their

backsides!"

Zap's wings drooped when he realised it was his turn next. "How can a tiny weevil like me attack a bigger creature?" he asked.

Gonzo smiled. "You'll see. Just remember your barrel roll."

The grasshopper made a loud click. Zap watched as a nearby bluebell began swaying. Then out of it flew his friend, Stripes the bumblebee.

"Quick – imagine Stripes is about to attack you," said Gonzo.

Stripes flew towards Zap. Buzzing filled his ears. He gulped when he

saw the bee's sharp stinger. But,

just before Stripes got close enough

to use it, Zap flipped over. He flew

beneath Stripes, upside down, and

gave the bee's back leg a gentle nip.

"Great!" shouted Gonzo.

Stripes looked over his wings and

smiled at Zap. "Good job we were

only practising!" he buzzed, before

flying away.

Zap joined the others back on the rock, pleased he had passed his test.

"What about me?" cried Lurch, jumping up and down, desperate for his turn.

Gonzo smiled. "You can use your great sense of smell," he said.

"To find lumps of poo to throw at attackers?" asked Lurch, excited.

"No, you can pick up the scent of strangers," replied Gonzo. "See if you can find one now."

Zap watched as Lurch landed on

a nearby rock. With his head close to

the ground, the dung beetle began to

sniff about. It wasn't long before his

head bounced up.

"Over there!" Lurch shouted,

pointing to a pile of dry leaves.

An insect with a long body and

loads of legs emerged from the

leaves.

"Wow," said Zap, impressed. "You

found a millipede!"

"Well done," said Gonzo. "This is my

29

old friend, Mazie. She's going to help you guard the wood."

Zap and his friends smiled at Mazie but she didn't smile back. Her face was wrinkled with worry as she rushed towards Gonzo.

"I've got some bad news," she said. "Some baby frogs have disappeared!"

Zap gasped. "That sounds like Spinner's work."

"It may not be," said Gonzo. "I'm afraid there are other enemies out there as well."

But Zap was sure it was Spinner.

30

There was no doubt about it. The spider was on the attack again and no one was safe.

CHAPTER 3

The Bug Buddies settled down for
the night beside Algae Pond, near to
where the frogs slept. The missing
babies still hadn't been found and
Zap was determined not to let
Spinner snatch any more. Lurch's
head lay on his squidgy dung ball.

32

Zap, Buzz and Crunch waited until
he'd closed his eyes before crawling
away from his stinky pillow.

Soon, Zap was listening to the
snores of his sleeping friends. But
as he gazed up at the full moon, Zap
was wide awake. If he couldn't even
find and save the baby frogs, how
would he ever be able to look after
the whole of Spinner's Wood?

Zap twisted and turned, unable to
rest. He looked up and saw Gonzo
watching him from his rock.

"Don't be nervous, Zap," said

 **33**

Gonzo. "Believe in yourself and you can do anything."

Zap closed his eyes – comforted because Gonzo believed in him. But as he began finally drifting off to sleep, he heard a hissing voice whisper:

Hungry, hungry, hungry me,
Wants a tasty snack for free.
Which new insect shall it be –
Cricket, fly or bumblebee?

Am I dreaming? thought Zap. *Or is that voice real?* But he was too tired

34

from his flying antics to find out, and soon he was falling asleep, curled up under a leaf. *Must have been a dream,* he thought…

Dawn broke and it was time for Gonzo to leave. The bugs waved their wings as they watched their friend hop away on his journey.

"I'd like to go to Cowpat Pasture one day," said Lurch. "A **whole field** full of fresh poo. Think of how many dung balls I could make!"

As soon as Gonzo was out of sight, Zap hovered in the air.

"Right, let's start our rounds," he said.

"We haven't had breakfast yet!" cried Buzz.

"No time," shouted Zap, darting off into the trees. "We've got a wood to protect – and some baby frogs to find."

All was peaceful as they flew around Spinner's Wood. The other insects were tucking into their breakfast. Crunch's stag beetle friends were licking sap from some tree bark. The snail squad were gobbling up green leaves. Sadly, there was no sign of the baby frogs, but Zap refused to give up hope.

Zap smiled as he heard a loud rumble come from Buzz's stomach.

"Please can we stop for some food soon?" the ladybird begged. **"I'm feeling dizzy!"**

37

"OK," said Zap. "After we've

checked on the baby grasshoppers."

They found them in a clearing,

clinging to a grass stalk. The hot

sun made their bodies

shine.

"They're just

like mini-Gonzos!"

said Crunch.

"We should get them

in the shade," said Zap.

"The sun is dangerous for

their skin."

The Bug Buddies flew down towards the young grasshoppers. But Crunch had such a wobbly landing that he nearly knocked the babies off the stalk. Zap quickly looked around to check that no one was hurt, and spotted something shiny out of the corner of his eye. A line of silk threaded through the grass...

Zap gulped – Spinner had been here. Was he planning to eat the baby grasshoppers, too?

CHAPTER 4

"Quick!" Zap cried. **"It's not safe here."**

"We're too tired to move," one of the baby grasshoppers mumbled. "The sun has made us sleepy."

Zap pointed to the silk trailing along the ground beside them. "If you don't move, you'll all end up in Spinner's stomach!"

With that, the babies agreed to move – quick sharp! The Bug Buddies helped to guide them as they waddled through the grass. Zap soon found a new home for them in the shady plants surrounding Soggy Bog.

"You'll be much safer here," he said.

The baby grasshoppers settled down to rest after their fright. Buzz, Lurch and Crunch huddled around Zap, looking worried.

 41

"What shall we do?" whispered Buzz. "Spinner won't give up easily."

Zap thought for a moment, hearing Gonzo's voice in his head.

Believe in yourself and you can do anything.

Zap knew what he had to do.

"I have to track down Spinner," he said.

Crunch's giant antlers shuddered with fright. **"Are you bonkers!"**

"I've got to

let him know *we're* in charge, not the other way around," said Zap.

Lurch stood as tall as he could manage. "Then we'll come too," he said.

"No," Zap replied. "I'll be quicker by myself."

Before his friends could argue, Zap took off, whizzing between the blades of grass as he followed the silky web deep into the forest. He shivered as the air around him cooled. He'd entered Shadow Creek – the scariest place in the whole wood.

Suddenly, Zap noticed that the light had disappeared. It was almost pitch black. *It can't be night-time already,* he thought. Then he realised it was a shadow. And Zap knew there was only one thing that could cast a shadow *that* big...

Zap gulped and looked up. An enormous black body and eight hairy legs dangled menacingly above him.

Spinner!

He froze as the giant spider crawled up the glistening thread towards his home in an old oak tree.

Now's my chance to warn him off, Zap thought, trying to fill his tiny body with courage.

He flew towards Spinner. Up close, he could see the spider's hairy legs. *They're big enough to squash me!* Zap realised. He shook his head and flapped his wings hard – he could not show fear. He *had* to be brave.

Zap was right underneath Spinner

now. He zoomed in and gave the

spider's fat stomach a nip as he flew

past.

Spinner span round, hissing with anger. He stared at Zap, baring his sharp fangs. "That'll be the last time you ever bite anyone," the spider hissed.

Spinner pushed himself off a branch and lunged forwards. But Zap was too quick, flying up to a safe height.

"And that's the last time **YOU** pick on any baby frogs," Zap shouted back.

"Frogs?" said Spinner, smiling. "I haven't been near any frogs."

"Yeah, right," said Zap. "And leave the baby grasshoppers alone, too **or else!**"

But Spinner only chuckled, before slowly crawling back up the tree.

Zap watched the spider disappear, and then zipped away. He'd done it – he'd faced up to Spinner! And he'd forced the nasty spider to back down.

Now he'll think twice before attacking smaller creatures, Zap thought, smiling.

Back at Soggy Bog, his friends cheered his return. But, as Zap flew down to join them, he noticed Mazie the millipede was frowning.

"What's wrong?" asked Zap.

"Another baby frog has gone missing," she said, holding back a sob.

Zap was shocked.

"It can't have been Spinner," he said. "I was just with him."

The friends all shared a worried look.

"Oh no," said Zap. "It looks like there are *more* enemies out there!"

CHAPTER 5

The Bug Buddies flew around Soggy

Bog, searching for any fierce-looking

beetles. Mazie crawled along the

ground, searching for bug prints.

None of them found any sign of

strangers.

Zap hovered above the baby

grasshoppers, who were lying still in the shade on the edge of the bog. *Very still*. Zap frowned. He zoomed down towards them and saw that the young grasshoppers were breathing – but they weren't moving at all.

"Something's happened to the babies!" he shouted.

His friends flew down to join him. "It's like they're sleeping with their eyes open," Lurch whispered.

"Hey kids," said Buzz, "first one to count my spots gets to ride Crunch around Soggy Bog three times!"

But the grasshoppers didn't move
at all.

A gentle breeze blew over the
bog. Lurch's antennae lifted into the
air.

53

"I can smell something by the willow tree," he said, lifting himself up into the air. "Or *someone*," added Crunch, nervously.

The three friends followed Lurch as he tracked the scent. Mazie crawled after them. The Bug Buddies finally stopped right underneath the drooping willow.

"Phew," said Crunch, looking around. "No nasty bugs here."

Zap looked up at the sagging branches. A green stick suddenly came to life, leaping out of the tree and swiping at him. Zap only just had time to beetle-flip out of the way.

"What was that?" he cried, as his attacker flew back into the tree.

"Oh no!" said Mazie. **"It's a praying mantis!** She was camouflaged among the branches. Those things are deadly!"

Zap squinted to see better. The praying mantis hid among the leaves. Its green body was long and thin, and it had six skinny legs. The front two were bent up next to each other under its chin. Huge green eyes stared down at Zap.

55

"Be careful," warned Mazie. "She'll eat anything that moves. But first she bites her prey to paralyse it!"

Zap locked eyes with the praying mantis. He suddenly felt more angry than afraid. "So," he said, "it's *your* fault the baby grasshoppers can't move."

"That's right," hissed the mantis.

"But why don't you come a little closer? I can't hear you too well…"

Crunch's antlers clattered together as he trembled with fear. **"She's going to freeze-i-fy us!"** he cried.

Zap gathered his friends in a huddle, talking quietly so the praying mantis could not hear. "We need to

distract her," he said. "We need
to give the babies enough time to
recover from the effects of her bite
before she gives them any more."

"But she looks almost as nasty as
Spinner," said Lurch. "How are we
going to do that?"

Zap felt himself smile. "With Bug
Attack moves, of course!" he said.

"Yeah!" said Buzz, suddenly flying
towards the praying mantis. The
ladybird hurled jets of poison at her
long body, but it didn't seem to have
any effect.

Crunch then did a great job flying crazily in front of the evil insect. Her head circled around and around as she watched the unsteady stag beetle. Zap could see the praying mantis was getting very dizzy. *Perhaps a nasty nip will send this evil insect on her way*, he thought. Just like it did with Spinner.

Enemy Attack!

He darted upwards, hiding behind the drooping branches. But as he got close enough to bite, the praying mantis quickly swivelled her head towards him. Faster than he could flap his wings, she grabbed him with her spiky front legs and bit into his neck!

The world suddenly became very blurry.

The rhyme Zap had heard in his dream came hissing back to him.

Hungry, hungry, hungry me…

And everything went black.

CHAPTER 6

Zap woke up from a deep sleep. He heard the rustling noises of the wood around him. *I'm alive*, he thought, *but why can't I move my wings?* He slowly opened his eyes. **Oh no!** He was in the worst place possible – **trapped in one of Spinner's webs!**

Enemy Attack!

*The praying mantis must have dragged
me here after she bit me,* he thought.
She and Spinner are working as a team!
Zap shivered as he heard his attacker's
hissing voice followed by Spinner's
rasping one. They were below him on
the web – and they were arguing.

"I'm eating the weevil's body,"
hissed the mantis. "You
can have his legs."

"No, Camolo," snarled Spinner. "I should get to eat his body. He's trapped in *my* web."

"Only because *I* bit him," the praying mantis replied. "I caught the weevil! You tried that once, Spinner – and **you failed!**"

Zap's whole body was trembling. He didn't want any part of him to get eaten – by anyone! He pulled against the sticky strands, but he was bound up too tight. Camolo whipped her head round towards him.

"Ah ha! Looks like our prisoner has

woken up," she said.

Spinner looked at Zap, with an evil

smile on his face.

"You can't bite me now, little

weevil," he said.

"But we can bite *you*," said Camolo, hissing with glee.

"You won't make a big meal," laughed Spinner, "but you look very tasty."

Zap shuddered as the two predators crawled towards him. He quickly thought back to his Bug Attack moves training. But how would that help him now his wings were tied up?

His attackers were getting closer, hungry for their meal. Zap looked desperately around for a way to

escape. Then he spotted something
in the tree opposite. A giant set of
antlers… seven spots… a dung ball
being rolled along a branch… His
friends had come to rescue him!

Enemy Attack!

Zap wanted to cry out in delight. But he knew he couldn't give them away, or their rescue plan wouldn't work.

Zap looked back at the web to see his attackers getting ready to pounce. Spinner licked his sharp fangs… Camolo stretched out her spiky legs… Zap's heart pounded. He hoped that his Bug Buddies had a good rescue plan.

If they didn't, Spinner and Camolo would have a *very* big dinner. All four of them!

CHAPTER 7

It was down to Zap to think of

something to distract the evil pair.

He couldn't let them see the other

Bug Buddies until they launched their

surprise attack.

"Hey," he called out, "don't you

dumbos know you should eat clover

seed weevils with a few leaves of
clover? Why don't you go and find
some?"

Spinner and Camolo burst out
laughing.

"Do we look like plant eaters?"
hissed Camolo.

"Why eat grass when
there are so many
delicious bugs?"
said Spinner.

The web shook as their big bodies
trembled with laughter.

"Enough joking," said Spinner,
eventually. **"It's dinner time!"**

Camolo and the giant spider took one final step towards Zap. But they had been so busy sniggering, they hadn't noticed the other Bug Buddies spring into action from the nearby tree. Or the large conker that was flying towards them.

"**Ow!**" shouted Camolo, as the spiky missile hit her on the head.

"That's for biting our friend!" shouted Buzz.

Spinner hissed angrily as he turned to see the Bug Buddies pulling back twigs to send more conkers soaring

72

their way. The spiky balls tore huge

holes in the web. Camolo and Spinner

tried to scramble to safety, but the

strands ripped and the web fell apart.

Zap, Camolo and Spinner slipped though the holes and plunged towards the forest floor.

I'm going to get splattered! Zap thought, closing his eyes tight as the ground got closer and closer.

But, instead of going *splat*, he went *boing* as he landed on something soft. Zap opened his eyes to see that Mazie the millipede had crawled to the rescue and curled up in a ball for Zap to bounce off.

Spinner wasn't so lucky. He landed on the ground with a loud *crunch*.

Camolo had even less luck. She'd landed with a **squelch** – right on top of Lurch's dung ball!

Zap gave a little smile as the stinky mantis ran off into the undergrowth,

75

twisting and turning round and round as she struggled to shake the poo off her back. All eight of Spinner's eyes glared at Zap as he clambered to his feet.

"One day, little weevil," he snarled, as he limped off after Camolo.

Buzz, Lurch and Crunch flew down to Zap.

"Yippee, you're OK," cheered Buzz.

"Only thanks to my Bug Buddies," replied Zap.

Lurch looked at what was left of his squished dung ball.

"Sorry about Ploppy," said Zap, patting Lurch on the back with his wing.

"It's all right," replied the dung beetle. "I can always get another dung ball, but I can't get another best friend."

Zap's tiny body filled with happiness – his Bug Buddies were the best. But his smile fell away when he heard Spinner's angry voice call out from inside the wood.

"Come back, Camolo," he cried. "What about our plan?"

Enemy Attack!

"What plan?" asked Buzz.

Lurch gasped. "Oh no! Are they going to eat the baby grasshoppers?"

Zap shook his head. "It's OK," he said. "Spinner and Camolo are heading in the wrong direction. The babies are safe. But just in case, let's go check on them."

He flapped his wings and took to the air. His friends were at his side in a flash.

"Back to Soggy Bog!" Zap cried.

CHAPTER 8

The Bug Buddies flew fast through
Spinner's Wood. Soggy Bog finally
came into view, and so did lots of tiny
little shapes – the baby grasshoppers!
They were moving again and Gonzo
was with them! He must have come
back early from Cowpat Pasture.

"Are the babies all right?" Zap asked, as he landed next to the wise grasshopper.

"Sleepy, but fine," said Gonzo. "Apart from this one, who still won't move."

Zap looked at the baby grasshopper, still frozen from Camolo's bite.

"I've got an idea," he said. He flapped his wings as hard as he could, fanning some air over the baby's face. The other

Bug Buddies quickly joined in. The cool breeze soon woke the little grasshopper, who slowly hopped over to his friends.

"Well done, all of you," said Gonzo, smiling. But then he frowned, looking at the baby grasshoppers. "What happened to them? Why are they moving so slowly?"

Zap told Gonzo about Camolo, the baby frogs and the Bug Buddies' group attack on Spinner's web.

"We showed that mean old spider," said Buzz, proudly.

Gonzo was quiet as he took it all in.
Suddenly, Mazie crawled through the
grass looking very happy... followed
by the missing baby frogs!

"The frogs are OK," she said.
"Camolo bit them then hid their
bodies over at Rotten Row. But Stripes
the bumblebee found them and

stood guard until they'd all woken up."

Gonzo smiled at Zap. "Looks like I could have stayed away a bit longer," he said.

Zap smiled back, delighted his friend was pleased with him.

Crunch, Buzz and Lurch crawled off to play with the babies. Zap was about to join them when he remembered Spinner's last words.

"Spinner said something about having a plan," said Zap, worried. "What do you think it is?"

Gonzo shook his head, sadly. "Spinner used to be in charge of this wood," he said. "That's where it got its name from. There is just one thing Spinner wants…"

Gonzo didn't finish his sentence. Zap guessed what he was going to say. *Spinner wants to control the wood again*, he thought.

Gonzo smiled, changing the subject.

"But look what one little weevil can

do when he believes in himself," he

said. "You're ready for anything

85

Spinner and his allies get up to now."

Zap looked across at Buzz,
Crunch and Lurch as they carried
the babies around on their
shoulders. *Gonzo's right,* he thought.
With the Bug Buddies by my
side, I can do anything!

CLOVER SEED
WEEVIL

NAME: Zap

FAMILY: Curculionidae

SIZE: 3 mm

HOME: canopy of Spinner's Wood

LIKES: Beetle Ball, flying, fresh leaves, helping other bugs

DISLIKES: Spinner, mean bugs, being small

ZAP

Clover seed weevils like moving around at night (nocturnal) or on cloudy days. Otherwise they're a bit timid and like to hang out amongst leaves. That makes Zap one very special weevil!

Young weevils (pupae) become adults in May/June, eat lots and then snooze! In autumn they wake up and lay their own eggs.

DUNG BETTLE

NAME: **Lurch**

FAMILY: **Scarabaeidae**

SIZE: **2 cm**

HOME: **the stinkiest parts
of Spinner's Wood**

LIKES: **fresh poo, rolling dung
balls**

DISLIKES: **cobwebs, dung ball
thieves**

LURCH

Dung beetles bury nearly half a ton of dung per acre per year as food!

There are around 7000 different species of dung beetle, and many specialise in different kinds of dung. That's a lot of beetles and a lot of poo!

Dung Beetles live in every continent except Antarctica. That's over a thousand species per continent!

Sainsbury's
Reading Scheme

CERTIFICATE
of Reading

My name is

_____

I have read

_____

Date

_____